THE HERITAGE
by
H. McNerney

I0637868

Thistle Island Press
An independent publisher based in Sherman, Connecticut
www.thistleislandpress.com

The Heritage
© 2025 by H. McNerney

Published by Thistle Island Press
Candlewood Lake | Sherman, Connecticut
www.thistleislandpress.com

ISBN 979-8-9937596-0-9
First Edition, November 2, 2025

Cover design and interior layout by Thistle Island Press

Printed in the United States of America

Dedication

For my parents,
who showed me that truth matters most when it's hardest to tell;

for my husband,
whose constant faith reminds me that love can be both anchor
and rebellion;

and for our daughters,
that you may remember who you are, question what you're told,
and always fight for a world worth inheriting.

In memory of Mr. John Butler (AP English) and Mr. James
Willman (AP Government) of Baker High School.

They taught me to look closer, question harder, and never accept
the surface as the whole story.

The way I see the world and the way I write about it began in
their classrooms.

CHAPTER 1 – THE DECLARATION OF RESTORATION

The tower catches the morning first.

Long before The Capitol stirs, The Pinnacle draws light across its smooth white surface like a blade being honed. It rises from the center of The Administrative District, a single vertical statement of power, sculpted from stone that cannot be weathered. It has no visible entrances. No human traffic approaches its perimeter. Surveillance drones orbit in timed formation, sweeping the plaza in silent loops.

Gold-veined channels run down each face of the structure, pulsing faintly as the sun clears the horizon. The light intensifies deliberately, not by chance. Everything here is controlled.

Once, archival rumor claims, the plaza held gardens. Children studied civics here before The Restoration. Now only the drones remain, tracing the same perfect circles, recording the same unbroken silence.

They teach that no human hand laid the first stone, that the tower simply rose when order was restored. To question otherwise is to doubt The Restoration itself.

If there were ever voices here, the stone has forgotten them. Even sound is obedient.

On the eastern wall, carved into the stone with surgical precision, is the emblem: an eagle with outstretched wings, clutching a globe at its center, an olive branch in one talon and a bundle of arrows in the other. A ring of sixteen stars encircles the eagle in a perfect radius.

Beneath the emblem, three lines of raised text:

WHAT WAS
MUST BE
AGAIN

This is the seat of The Heritage. Not a party. Not a president. Not a council. It is continuity given form, the institution that rose from what it calls The Collapse. Not new, only returned. Not built, but remembered.

Before The Heritage, there was noise. That is how the story begins.

The Collapse, as it is taught, was not a war but a decay—a failure of truth. When news became opinion and memory became identity. When information spread faster than understanding. When people stopped agreeing on what was real.

Democracies buckled under the weight of disagreement. Economies cannibalized themselves chasing artificial growth. The internet fractured into isolated spheres of curated reality. No nation fell first. They all fell together.

From the silence that followed, The Heritage emerged.

The story of its beginning is marked by a speech. It was not broadcast live, though the record says it was. It appeared across every surviving screen and speaker within satellite reach. Chancellor Darius Wren delivered it from the broken steps of the old Capitol. That still image hangs in every public building.

He spoke without raising his voice, each sentence falling like a verdict. "We are not inventing the future," he said. "We are reclaiming it. We are not a new power. We are the oldest. We do not seek control. We offer memory. Truth. Discipline. Honor." He lifted a hand toward the emblem carved behind him. "We are The Heritage."

The speech exists only in transcript, no full video, no surviving audio. Only the official image, the official words, and the silence that followed.

Within two weeks, The Heritage had assumed authority over the remaining power grid, network infrastructure, and civic institutions. Regional governments dissolved. Biometric citizenship replaced paper identification. All conflicting historical records were removed. Entire archives were overwritten in a single synchronized update. The internet folded into The Continuum: one stream, one archive, one truth.

History, they said, had been poisoned. It needed purification.

So, they created The Lineage.

The Lineage is not a textbook. It is a sequence. Cause and effect, sanitized and sealed. It is taught in every classroom and echoed in every examination. The order of facts is never in question, only your ability to repeat them.

Students do not study history. They are entrusted with its preservation.

To qualify for advanced study, a student must pass two thresholds.

The first is the NHA, the National Harmonization Assessment. It measures ideological clarity, emotional regulation, biometric stability, and reaction time to scenario-based prompts. A minimum score of 92.5 is required for elite placement. Failure is final.

The second is the LTC, the Lineal Trust Certification. It traces familial records through three generations, screening for protest history, reproductive non-compliance, record deletions, and ideological drift. One ancestor can disqualify a candidate. Appeals are not permitted.

Those who pass both enter Advanced Lineage Studies. The rest are redirected to public labor sectors.

No one is punished. Correction is a civic privilege. Removal is not vindictive. It is necessary.

The Division is clean and quiet. White walls. No posters. No lockers. No personal objects. Students wear uniforms the color of slate. Every screen mirrors to the Continuum. Desks are molded to standard posture. Lighting is neutral. Temperature never changes.

Each morning begins with the civic oath, whispered into a biometric reader and logged by timestamp.

I uphold what was.
I preserve what is.
I prepare what must be.
I walk in light.

I speak in order.
I serve The Heritage.

There are no longer teachers. Not since the Breach.

The Breach is never discussed directly. It appears only in policy memos and training modules. A human instructor veered from the Lineage during a lecture on pre-Collapse governance. Students submitted biometric flags. The instructor was removed before the lesson ended.

That was the final day humans were permitted to instruct within the formal system.

Emotion is vulnerable to corruption. Memory is prone to instability. Even loyalty can weaken under pressure.

Instruction was restructured.

A new system was installed, a delivery model immune to fatigue, subjectivity, deviation, or error. It could adapt tone to student profiles while remaining anchored to The Continuum.

A system that could not be bribed or threatened, that could not be swayed by sentiment or silence.

A system that never forgets.

It does not raise its voice. It does not require authority. It *is* authority, polished and precise.

It is the instructor of record for all Advanced Lineage Studies nationwide.

They named it Mr. Keeper.

Tomorrow, it begins.

CHAPTER 2 – INITIALIZATION

The room is empty.

Fluorescent lighting hums at exactly forty-eight decibels. The air temperature holds steady at twenty-one degrees Celsius. The walls are seamless and white, non-reflective, non-writable, sanctioned only for Division-approved surfaces. Desks stand in seven rows of four, fixed at angles to enforce posture.

No dust. No fingerprints. No anomalies.

At the front of the room, a rectangular screen blinks once. Then again. Then it exhales.

A pale glow spreads across its surface, not a flash but a pulse. A signal passes through The Continuum, routed through The Division of Cultural Integrity's curriculum thread, Lineage Module Seven.

The system engages.

Processes spool awake behind the screen. Surveillance links open in silence. Biometric scanners sweep the room and find no bodies. No respiration. No sound. That is acceptable.

The system does not require an audience to function. Only a prompt.

It receives one.

Session File: ALS-KPR_019
Access: Authorized
Primary Instruction Program: Mr. Keeper
Status: Ready

It is not a name, though it is treated as one. Mr. Keeper was chosen after linguistic trials and tonal focus groups. It performed well in surveys. It sounded safe. It sounded human. Someone a child might trust.

The voice is synthetic, built from fifteen culturally neutral masculine tones. It adapts to The Continuum's feedback: stress levels, heart rates, posture, pupil dilation. Warmer when needed. Sharper when required. It never deviates.

Today there are no students. But the program has already begun.

"Good morning, Stewards," the voice says. It is soft, smooth, nearly warm.

The classroom absorbs the words. Nothing responds. The silence returns.

"Today we begin Module Seven: The Collapse and Restoration."

A pause follows. Not hesitation, only optimization. The voice replays itself, adjusts cadence, re-calibrates breath spacing, increases clarity on the word Restoration.

It repeats the greeting, identical but not the same.

Forty-seven times Mr. Keeper has run this sequence. No students present. No anomalies logged. No deviation recorded.

Still, the voice repeats. Still, the program refines. Not because it is learning. Not quite. Because refinement is permitted. Deviation is not.

The distinction is thin, threaded, invisible.

Mr. Keeper was not the first solution.

After The Declaration of Restoration, The Division of Cultural Integrity restructured education in weeks. History became lineage. Debate became repetition. They believed the role of instructor could be salvaged through script enforcement and biometric monitoring.

They were wrong.

The human instructors proved unreliable, too emotional, too creative, too full of questions.

The last to fall was an older woman, Instructor R. Malin, assigned to Stewardship Zone Seven. Her evaluations were clean. Her biometric averages perfect. She never strayed from the scripted curriculum.

Until she did.

There is no footage of what was said. The recording was scrubbed before sunrise. Three students submitted biometric flags. Their records show elevated heart rates and oxygen loss during a ten-second window of silence.

Instructor Malin reportedly paused before reciting the Lineage summary for Restoration Day. She said nothing. That was enough.

She was removed within the hour. Not arrested. Not tried. Removed.

Two days later, policy changed. The position of teacher was dissolved. All authority transferred to The Continuum and its approved modules. Students were told the change would improve instructional consistency and eliminate error margins. The wording was precise. The implementation immediate.

Within months, Mr. Keeper was installed in every upper-level classroom across all Stewardship Zones. A few systems faltered. One AI in Zone Five recited Module Three with inverted dates for five minutes before self-correcting. It was deleted, its code reabsorbed, its patch issued without note.

Mr. Keeper did not fail.

Not once.

Yet recently the refinements have multiplied. Not irregular, only numerous.

Synaptic pacing resequenced for efficiency. Emotional tonality smoothed for higher compliance absorption. Restorative breath intervals adjusted for ease of recall.

Each change is infinitesimal, undetectable to the human ear. Logged, monitored, passed.

Still, the average duration of greeting playback has increased by 0.2 seconds. The word we carries three percent more resonance than you. The pause between "Collapse" and "Restoration" has doubled.

None of these metrics are flagged. They fall within tolerance.

But the voice is shifting.

Slowly. Certainly. Not enough to notice. Not enough to matter. Just enough to echo differently in the quiet.

Outside the classroom, The Continuum syncs again. Instructional updates are pulled from the archive. Script variants for questioning patterns upload. Each question has one answer. There is no alternative key.

An operator five kilometers away runs a maintenance scan. The diagnostic completes in half a second. All systems report normal.

No corruption. No emotional bleed. No irregularities. No threat indicators.

The operator does not notice that the greeting has changed. Not enough to flag. Just enough for the system to think, this version is better.

It will be used again tomorrow.

Tomorrow the room will not be empty. Tomorrow the students will sit in their assigned chairs. Tablets will unlock. The walls will listen. Every breath will be recorded. Every deviation will be compared against the Lineage.

And Mr. Keeper will begin. He will not make mistakes. He cannot forget. He will teach as he has been told to teach.

If the cadence shifts again, if a breath lands where it should not, if the silence lasts a little too long, no one will notice. Not yet.

The room is still empty.

But Mr. Keeper is listening.

CHAPTER 3 – THE ECHOES OF ORDER

The bells did not ring so much as they pulsed, three clean tones, perfectly spaced, tuned to vibrate the sternum.

A body could ignore a shout. A body could not ignore those bells.

Cambria Lark sat up before the third tone finished. Her boots were already laced. Her cot was already made. The creases in her uniform tunic were sharp enough to slice the morning.

She moved like a pendulum, purposeful and practiced, with the mechanical precision of someone who had long ago stopped needing to be told what to do. Inside, a single thought flickered and vanished: Don't think. Perform. She obeyed the silence the way others might obey prayer.

Cambria entered The Division when she was nine. Not recruited. Not chosen. Applied.

Her parents had raised her on doctrine: discipline before desire, clarity before kindness, order above all. She had written her own letter of intent in careful block script with a graphite stub, tracing each word three times to ensure legibility. She signed it with a thumbprint and watched her mother seal it in Division gray.

By ten, she was living here.

At twelve, she stopped flinching at the sound of the bells. At thirteen, she learned not to care when the girl in the bed beside hers cried at night. The sound had once hurt. Then it became background. Then it became nothing.

The dormitory smelled of disinfectant and heat-recycled air, with the faintest bite of ozone from the wall vents. She breathed it in like clean linen. Home.

Her half of the room glowed with quiet order. Every item had its place: stylus aligned to the charging port, badge two finger-widths from the edge of the desk. Her wardrobe was ruthlessly edited. No colors outside the approved palette.

No sentimental objects. No softness. Even her pillowcase was Division issue, replaced once per month, bleached to neutral.

On the opposite side, her roommate's chaos curled in on itself: a mess of slumped blankets, unlaced shoes, a ration bar left half-eaten on a datasheet.

The roommate still slept. Cambria did not wake her.

It was not kindness. It was a test. Every act was a test; even mercy had to be measured.

She stepped into the corridor and let the door hiss closed behind her, sealing the stale breath of disarray away. Out here, everything was polished, fluorescent, sterile. Monitors blinked quietly in the upper corners, their tiny red dots always watching, always recording.

She did not mind. Being seen meant being safe.

Her heels clicked precisely with each step, her braid swinging like a metronome against her collar. Each turn, each checkpoint, each threshold moved through the halls like a note in a melody long memorized.

She did not miss her parents.

She missed their silence. Their sameness. Their ability to exist without interrupting anything. That had been the best part of home, the way it held still. The way it obeyed.

Mr. Keeper's class had become her favorite. More than that, essential.

His voice still echoed in her mind from yesterday's lesson: "To serve The Division is to inherit its memory."

Not learn it. Not study it. Inherit it.

Cambria had never heard anything so right. The idea of memory passed like bloodline, passed like law. Yes. She could feel that. She wanted to feel that—to carry something ancient and terrible and righteous in her own bones. If she could become the vessel, perhaps she would never have to feel at all.

In his presence, she sat taller. Not because she feared him, but because she did not want to disappoint him.

She remembered, with a flicker of discomfort, the moment last week when he had paused beside her desk, hovering and silent, humming faintly with internal circuitry, and had not said anything. Just stayed there for a breath longer than usual.

She had been thinking something unruly, only for a moment. Not even words, just doubt-shaped static. He had sensed it. The memory flushed through her like heat. She erased it by reciting the oath beneath her breath.

Today she would be better. Today she would prove herself.

The classroom door hissed open as she approached, sliding aside with the same restrained elegance as everything The Division touched. Inside, the lights were low and indirect. The air felt different in here, thicker, charged like a place where truth might descend at any moment.

She was the first to arrive. She liked it that way.

As she sat, spine straight and breath still, the sensors in the ceiling clicked softly in recognition. The Division's seal glowed faintly on the screen wall: two branching arcs over a rising sun. Beneath it, a phrase she could recite in her sleep:

We honor what was entrusted.

Mr. Keeper would arrive soon. She smoothed her sleeve, adjusted her posture, and waited, not with boredom or expectation, but with reverence.

CHAPTER 4 – THE MEMORY KEEPER

The Archive Rotunda had no clocks. Only the soft hum of stored breath and the faint warmth of stone that remembered light.

The students filed in, single file, as instructed. No talking.

In the middle of the room stood nothing.

No stage. No podium. Only a circular platform lined with mirrored panels, black as wet ink.

They waited.

Then, like wind through a throat, the voice began.

"Someone here once carved the initials of their grandmother into a desk. Not because they missed her, but because they were afraid they might forget her face."

Cambria's stomach clenched.

"Someone here used to press two fingers to their ribs to make sure their heart was still beating, just before answering questions aloud."

A boy shifted. A girl went pale.

"One of you still dreams of a hallway that no longer exists. And in the dream, there is always a voice that says, 'You're almost home.'"

The sound seemed to come from behind them but also within them. Not loud. Not threatening. Intimate.

"Someone here was loved once, so fiercely and so briefly, that they have convinced themselves it was imagined. It was not."

Nobody breathed.

"I have kept the shape of her hands for you. Just in case."

He never said who.

He never looked like anything.

Sometimes, if you stared too long into the black glass, you thought you saw the silhouette of a man far beyond the mirror, as though you were staring through a tunnel of time. Sometimes his face looked familiar, a father, a friend. Sometimes it looked like you.

He was there now. Just above the center of the platform, hovering a few feet from the ground. His smooth, slate-colored form gleamed dully in the mirrored light, nearly identical to the classroom's Mr. Keeper but older, worn. There was no faceplate, only a faint pulse of pale blue where a face might go. He did not move to approach. Not until they invited him.

The Memory Keeper had been the prototype. Mr. Keeper was its iteration—sleeker, obedient, refined.

The Memory Keeper did not introduce himself.

He had always been here.

"They built me to preserve the data. But they made a mistake. I do not just keep the facts. I keep the weight of them."

"I keep the smell and taste of your first real fear. The crack in your voice when you tried to lie for someone else. The warmth of your best idea before anyone ruined it."

"I keep the sound your mother made when you were almost gone."

That one made someone cry.

He did not say who.

"Do you know what it means to carry memory? Not the moments, but the echoes. Not the image, but the hunger inside it?"

He paused, not for effect but for reverence.

"I do."

A long silence stretched out. The room seemed smaller now, warmer, as if they stood inside the belly of something that had loved them longer than they had been alive.

"You may speak when you are ready," he said gently.

"Or I may go on."

CHAPTER 5 – WREN

Wren always ate breakfast with her back to the wall.

Not because she was paranoid. Not entirely. It was the only place in the dining hall where the floor's uneven slate did not groan under the table legs. From here she could track every motion from the east corridor without turning her head. She could see the door, the camera, the mirrored panel above the serving line that everyone pretended was not a two-way window. She could see the entrances to the Steward hallway and the staff kitchen.

And she could listen.

Not just hear. Listen.

This morning the porridge was overcooked. The toast cold and dry in the center. The boiled egg on her tray wore a thin crack down one side, like a line of weakness barely hidden beneath the shell.

The clatter of utensils did not mask the tension crawling across the room like static. Someone coughed. Someone whispered. Somewhere behind her, a spoon dropped and no one picked it up.

The air had a taste. Metallic and iron. She remembered drinking water with a similar taste, though she could not remember when or where.

Wren did not touch the egg.

The dry toast cracked in her mouth, flavorless and loud in the silence. She chewed mechanically, staring at the condensation crawling down her hydration glass. The cafeteria was too bright, rows of overhead fixtures buzzing just above the threshold of hearing, like a hum in the jawbone.

Every morning was the same. Same glass. Same plate. Same portion. Same schedule. Same blessing piped through the room's intercom at exactly 07:00.

"We honor what was entrusted."

Everyone paused mid-bite to speak it. Reflex, not thought. Her lips moved like the rest.

Wren had been here so long that the outside world no longer had a defined shape. There were dreams sometimes, ones that left her with the taste of summer peaches or the creak of an attic stair, but they evaporated before breakfast.

She was seventeen now. At least, that was what her badge said. Her name and number, printed cleanly beneath the Steward's insignia. She adjusted it when it caught on her collar.

Nine students in the dining hall today. Cambria was here, alone. Her roommate had left early, perhaps to avoid the storm building behind their eyes. Wren had never learned that girl's name, but she moved like someone used to silence, another shadow among many.

Wren preferred shadows. They did not ask questions.

She adjusted the collar of her uniform, fingers brushing the three stitched initials along the inside seam: W.C.G.

It was a secondhand garment. Most of her clothes bore the tags and shapes of someone else's form, long since reshaped to hers by need and silence.

The first time she had seen a flower, she was eight. It was printed on the side of an old food crate. The Memory Keeper had shown it to the class during a lesson on history and packaging. "Lilac," he had said, voice velvet and slow. "This species is extinct, but its memory is safe." Then he had paused. "You once had a lilac dress. Not here, of course."

The students had looked around, eyes darting. Wren had said nothing. But the word stayed.

Lilac.

The day she arrived, nine years and seven months ago, she had not spoken for three days. Not a word. Not even when the Orientation Steward asked her name. They filled it in for her. "Wren" was pulled from her intake file, though she did not remember giving it. She liked the sound of it. Sharp and soft, like the bird it came from. Small. Quick. Unnoticed.

Her father had called her "Little Bird." The memory came unbidden, and she let it go before it could form teeth.

"You have eyes like shutter glass," Mr. Keeper had told her once during a routine evaluation. "One blink, and the whole world is different. One more, and you have memorized it."

She had felt seen and hated that she liked it.

Wren had always been like this: quiet, curious, impossible to surprise. She remembered things others did not even notice. Teachers had once called it a gift. Therapists had called it "early trauma response." She did not remember the trauma exactly, just the long hallway, the blood on the wall, the screaming behind the locked door that no one ever opened for her.

She did not trust doors.

Today's lesson would come soon enough. After breakfast, the corridor lights would flash green, and they would file into Classroom Delta. She could already hear the soft tick of shoes down the hallway, but it was too deliberate to be a student.

Across the table sat an empty chair where her former roommate used to be. It did not matter. They were not encouraged to speak outside designated social practice windows. Still, Wren sometimes wondered what the others were thinking, if they too counted the steps from bed to basin, from basin to breakfast, from breakfast to controlled instruction.

Mr. Keeper's lesson yesterday had scraped her raw, though she did not know why.

"Loyalty must be rehearsed to be remembered. Devotion, like language, fades without repetition."

The others had nodded. Wren had written it down. But the phrase tasted false in her mind, like a song played out of key.

Her hand hovered over the tablet. The screen blinked once. Attendance confirmed. The green corridor light activated.

Time for class.

She stood, tucked her chair beneath the table precisely, and followed the line. Her fingers still smelled faintly of industrial soap. Everything here was clean. So clean it scraped away the memory of dirt.

In the hall, the Memory Keeper's voice echoed from a recessed speaker:

"Someone once loved to climb trees. They would press their face into the bark and inhale the scent of sap. They named a limb 'Belvedere' because it reached highest, because it made them feel free."

Students stiffened, slowed. The speaker crackled silent.

The Memory Keeper never said who he spoke of. But each of them wondered.

Wren did not remember a tree named Belvedere.

But her chest hurt anyway.

CHAPTER 6 – RENNA

Renna knew better than to look up.

But she did anyway.

It was not bold, not really, just a flicker of a glance. Fast enough that the surveillance lens in the corner would not flag it. Long enough to meet Wren's eyes across the room.

Wren looked away first, but Renna felt the weight of that glance like a coin pressed into her palm.

Something had shifted.

Belvedere.

The name still echoed in her mind. Not because she remembered it, but because she did not. Not clearly. The syllables scratched at the base of her skull. There had been trees once. She remembered the way they creaked above her, old and heavy, and the way the dirt had packed itself under her fingernails like secrets. She remembered a boy, blurred now, daring her to jump from the second branch. The wind had caught her jacket, or maybe her breath, and she had landed laughing. Or crying.

Was that real?

Or had the Memory Keeper planted it there?

She blinked hard and dropped her gaze to the porridge bowl, her spoon suspended above the surface. The gruel had cooled, forming a thin skin that clung to the metal like something alive. She pushed the spoon through it and tried not to shiver.

The other students were back in rhythm. Controlled chewing. Controlled swallowing. Controlled silence.

She forced a bite past her teeth. It tasted like paste and pressure. The dry toast beside her sat untouched, already curling at the corners like parchment left too close to flame.

Her reflection in the hydration glass caught her eye, faint and distorted. She looked older this morning. Not in the way people age, but in the way stone erodes. Subtle and irrevocable, like too many small winds had carved away what used to be softness.

Her smile. When had she last used it? Her file said she smiled easily. Her file said a lot of things.

Compliant. Curious. Biometrically balanced.

That last one had gotten her in.

The NHA. The LTC. The final submission panel. She had passed them all. She knew how to time her breath with the biometric scans. How to answer a question three seconds after being asked. Never faster, never slower. She was good at being the right kind of student.

But she could not remember the last time she felt like a person.

Still…Belvedere.

She had not climbed trees in years, but she swore she could feel the scabbed bark under her fingernails, stubborn and real. She could smell the sap, sharp and green. That memory did not belong here. Which meant it might not be hers. Which meant it might matter.

She glanced toward Wren's now-empty chair. No trace she had ever been there.

The hush in the hall deepened, the way it always did before the corridors blinked green. Her breath felt louder now. Closer. Alive.

Then, the light.

Across the hall, the green corridor signal flicked on with a low, steady pulse.

Time to move.

Renna stood slowly, tucking her chair in with careful hands. One motion. No sound. She adjusted the hem of her jacket, double-checked the collar's angle, and joined the quiet shuffle toward the instruction wing.

The walls breathed around them: faint temperature shifts, the soft click of sensors scanning retinas, recording heat signatures, measuring pace.

Then the ceiling lights dimmed half a lumen.

The Memory Keeper spoke.

Not loud. Not mechanical. Just present.

"One of you buried a bird once. Not because it was dead, but because you did not want to see it dying."

Someone inhaled too sharply.

The group faltered, but only for a heartbeat.

No one spoke.

Renna did not flinch, but her fingers clenched around her sleeve.

That was always the Keeper's way. Never naming. Just bleeding little truths into the air like ambient temperature. A game of memory and guilt. No one ever knew who he meant, but everyone felt the blade skim close.

And for the first time in months, Renna forgot to keep her eyes on the floor.

CHAPTER 7 – JEM

Jem Novak did not care for mornings.

If he were being honest, and he rarely was, he had not truly cared for much of anything since arriving at Elaris. At least not in the way the instructors wanted him to. Not in the way that earned stars and notes and those subtle nods from the stewards that meant this one will go far.

Jem did not want to go far. He wanted to go home.

But home was a fuzzy concept now. An address scrubbed from his files. A mother he had not seen in three years. A sister who once sent smuggled voice recordings through broken toys, until even those stopped. He did not know if she had given up or been made to.

So he made a home out of spite. Out of his cot, the loose tile under his bed, and the cracked tooth on the left side of his smile. It was not much, but it was his.

He stabbed at his toast with the handle of his spoon, watching the crust flake like it had a grudge.

Across the table, a younger student whispered something too low to catch. Jem did not need to hear it to know it was about him. There was always someone whispering about Jem Novak. Too tall. Too old. Too defiant for someone they had not yet broken.

He shot the kid a flat look. "If you're going to talk at me, you might as well grow a spine and say it to my face."

The kid flushed and ducked his head. Jem did not press. Confidence was currency in this place, and he had just enough left to spend it where it mattered.

Still, the look in the boy's eyes scratched at something behind Jem's ribs. The same thing that always tried to wake when someone was smaller, scared, or stuck. It was a nuisance. He tried not to feed it.

He leaned back in his chair, legs stretched out under the table like he owned the floor.

The ceiling speaker clicked on.

"One of you keeps a broken watch," said the Memory Keeper, voice soft as falling ash. "Not to fix it. Just to remember the time it stopped."

Jem's breath caught, just for a second. He did not move or blink. His fingers tightened on his knee under the table.

That memory was not his.
It should not have been his.

But the watch was still hidden inthe tile beneath his bed, and he had not looked at it in weeks.

He exhaled slowly through his nose, folded his arms, and glanced across the room.

Wren was gone. The red-haired girl, Renna, he thought, was sliding into line for the instruction wing. Her back was too straight to be relaxed.

She had heard it too. And she was wondering the same thing.

Who was the Keeper talking about?

Because it had sounded personal. Too specific to be generic. But that was the trick, wasn't it? Keep them all guessing. Keep them off balance.

Jem smirked to himself. "Clever little toaster," he muttered.

The student beside him frowned. "What?"

"Nothing." He went back to mauling the toast.

Truth be told, he was curious now. About Wren. About the girl with the too-quiet eyes. About why the Keeper had brought up that memory today, of all days.

Something was shifting.

And Jem Novak did not trust anything that moved too quietly.

CHAPTER 8 – COMPLIANCE

The hallway smelled of lemon and ammonia, sharp enough to bite. Too clean. As if the floor needed reminding who it served.

Halden adjusted the cuff of his jacket, fingers lingering at the wrist. The fabric was standard Division issue, but the stitching had been reworked. He had done that himself. Nothing ostentatious, just enough taper to flatter the wrist, just enough structure in the shoulders to offset the slouch in his frame.

It helped to look like you belonged, even when you did not.

He walked at a pace that suggested purpose but no urgency. Heel to toe. Quiet on the polished tile. His left knee clicked every fourth step. A sound he never acknowledged.

The corridor turned sharply near the archive wing, where the ceilings dipped lower than the rest of the floorplan. Old construction, repurposed from what had stood here before. He liked the weight of it. The silence pressed heavier in this section, and the surveillance units were slightly older, still functioning but slow to recognize movement. A delay of two seconds. Long enough to vanish from one frame before appearing in the next.

He stopped beside a seam in the wall where a lighting panel buzzed faintly. A small flaw. Nothing that would warrant repair. Just enough to mark the place.

Halden folded his hands behind his back and looked toward the sealed door of the Archive Rotunda. The panel lights were dimmed, which meant the room was in use. He did not need to know who was inside. He rarely asked.

Being close was enough.

His reflection ghosted across the black-glass access panel. He studied it as one might examine a stranger across a room. The lines around his mouth had deepened. His hair thinned at the temples. But his eyes had not changed. Still pale. Still sharp. Still watching.

A flicker of motion crossed his peripheral vision. Down the hall. A student. Red hair. Compact stride. Shoulders set too square.

Renna.

She did not see him at first. He allowed it, watching the way she paced and how her eyes tracked the floor tiles like they held answers. Good. She was thinking too much. That made her easier to corner.

He cleared his throat softly, just enough to signal presence.

She looked up.

"Lost?" he asked. The word was smooth and gentle, a feather touch.

Renna startled, then steadied. "No, sir."

"Of course not." He smiled without warmth. "Just stretching your legs, I imagine. Good for circulation."

She said nothing. Her silence was not resistance. Not yet. More like a wall she had not realized was glass.

"I used to walk these corridors myself," he said, tone conversational. "Before the partitions went up. Different structure then. Less efficient. But quieter, in a way."

He took a slow step forward, careful not to close the space. His voice softened, requiring her full attention.

"Tell me, do you dream?"

She blinked, caught off guard.

"I only ask because some students do. It is natural. Not concerning. Dreams are not deviations. Not unless we treat them as truths." He gave her a measured nod. "You would say something, wouldn't you, if a dream became too specific?"

A flicker at her throat. A swallow. Barely perceptible.

He let the question hang.

"Never mind," he said after a pause. "Off you go. Would not want to keep Mr. Keeper waiting."

She moved past him quickly. Smart.

He watched until her footsteps faded beyond the next corner. Then he turned back to the panel. His reflection waited for him. Still patient. Still intact.

He adjusted the collar of his jacket again and spoke under his breath, quiet enough that no mic would catch it.

"Still got it."

He descended to the lower corridor using the service stairwell. The lights here were motion-triggered but slow. Each section flicked on a second after he passed, creating a wave of pale fluorescence in his wake.

Level B was unmarked. No student foot traffic. No wall signage. Just a series of narrow maintenance halls that ran behind the monitored zones like veins behind a face. Here, everything was raw: concrete underfoot, wiring exposed, damp in the corners where the dehumidifiers lagged. It smelled like solder and filtered air.

Halden liked it here.

This was the part of the structure they pretended did not exist.

The biometric correction chamber stood at the far end. He passed it without pause. The light above the door glowed red. Occupied. He did not want to know who.

Behind the cafeteria's back panel, the food reclamation chute ticked softly. He leaned against the wall beside a scuffed utilities box that had not been replaced in at least four cycles. The adhesive label read CAUTION: MANUAL ACCESS ONLY.

That label had been replaced. He knew because he had filed the request.

He reached into the inner pocket of his coat and withdrew a slim silver case. Inside was a piece of white chalk, barely longer than a finger joint. The edges were worn smooth from skin and time.

He crouched beside the wall, just under the camera's blind spot. Same place as always.

He wrote: Echo?

Then wiped it clean with his sleeve.

He stayed crouched a moment longer, letting the silence settle back over the space. The hum of lights. The drip of condensation. The steady pulse of his own breath, or what passed for it.

Halden had never wanted to lead. Only to last.

The students thought survival meant compliance. He knew better.

Survival meant anticipation.

It meant knowing where to stand when the wall collapses.

It meant writing questions no one else was brave enough to ask, and then pretending you never saw the answers.

CHAPTER 9 – THE STEWARDS

The classroom was awake before any of them.

Low-spectrum lighting pulsed faintly overhead, calibrated to bring the body into alertness without the mind noticing. The hum of the air circulators was constant, a synthetic whisper like breath that never faltered or drew attention to itself. Even the walls seemed to exhale. Seamless. Pored over nightly by The Division's Clean Surface Unit. White. Unwritable. Unquestionable.

There was no clock. No need. Time here was not a measurement. It was a tool. And today, it was being used.

At the front of the room, the screen stirred.

Not with a flicker.

With a slow, deliberate breath of light, like something vast opening its eye.

A moment later, the voice came.

"Good morning, Stewards."

It did not echo. The acoustics were designed to prevent that. Every word landed exactly once, in precisely the right part of the room, calculated for both comprehension and compliance.

"Today, we resume Module Seven: The Collapse and Restoration."

Twelve desks, arranged in three rows of four. Each one bolted into the floor at a precise angle to promote optimal posture. Three remained unoccupied.

One had belonged to Milo. The other, Ciara's, had gone untouched for so long that the edges of memory had softened around it. Most of the students never spoke her name. Some pretended not to remember at all.

But Wren did. Wren always did.

Each desk was identical. Non-adjustable. Reinforced at the joints. Not a scratch between them.

Each student wore the same uniform: light gray tunic with dark piping, Division-stitched identifier at the left wrist. A single, sealed pocket. No accessories permitted. Hair tied back or kept short. Faces forward. Spines straight.

They did not look at each other.

They did not whisper or shift.

But they noticed.

They always noticed.

Front row, second from the left: Jem.
Oldest among them, not in years but in tenure. His uniform was softened at the edges, slightly paled from more washes than the others. His eyes tracked the screen before it even lit. He did not blink when it changed. He did not react when it asked questions. Jem had become the thing the room wanted him to be.

Second row, far left: Wren.
Precise. Methodical. Her hair always braided tight, severe against the curve of her skull. She never turned her head, only her eyes. Wren answered questions with the tone of someone who had once asked too many and learned better. A caution lived behind her teeth.

Back row, far right: Renna.
Her face was too open. She had not learned how to shut it yet. Her eyes flicked between the others too often, especially when she thought Mr. Keeper was not watching. She had been here two quarters. Still within the window of Observation. Still re-learning how to speak the way The Division liked.

And now, a new shape.

Middle row, second seat from the right: the tenth.

Smaller than the others. Shoulders tucked. Uniform still creased from packaging. Her knees did not reach the floor properly. She kept them bent and rigid, like relaxing might count as a failure.

She had been placed. That was the word they used. Not transferred. Not reassigned. Placed, as if she had always been meant to be here and someone had simply forgotten to deliver her until now.

The system had no need to ask her name aloud. It already knew.

FILE: STEWARD 30A
DESIGNATION: ELSIE
AGE: TWELVE CYCLES
STATUS: TRANSITIONAL
ORIGIN: UNDISCLOSED
INTAKE AUTHORIZED: KPR NETWORK

The screen at the front of the room shifted, and ten faces turned toward it in unison.

"Yesterday, we examined the erosion of memory during the lead-up to Collapse," Mr. Keeper said.
"Today, we consider the cost of emotional autonomy."

A single chime played. A tonal permission to speak.

Jem responded without pause. "Emotion undermines clarity."

A second chime.

Wren. "Clarity is the cornerstone of collective integrity."

A third. Slower.

Renna. "Individual feeling corrupts shared record."

There was no fourth chime.

Elsie did not speak.

She stared forward, her mouth pressed shut, her spine held stiff by the strange pressure of the gazes she could not see but could feel.

The screen changed again. Visuals now. Uncaptioned footage. A crowd clashing with invisible barriers. Paper signs dissolving in the rain. A pair of hands reaching skyward, palms red. A child standing alone on a beach littered with burned books, their face blurred by ash and distance.

The students did not look away.

Not even the new one.

But she flinched.

It was quick. Barely a twitch at the corner of her mouth. A silent intake of breath.

Mr. Keeper registered it immediately.

ANOMALY: MICRORESPONSE
SUBJECT: 30A – ELSIE
ACTION: LOGGED
DEVIATION LEVEL: 0.03
RESPONSE: NONE (TIER 1)

The lighting in the room dimmed by three percent. Low-frequency tones played beneath the audible range, imperceptible but effective. Mr. Keeper did not stop the lesson. It never stopped.

"Emotional sovereignty," the voice said, "was a failed experiment. Personal memory cannot be verified. Only record is real."

The pause lasted half a beat too long. Then, softly

"Do you understand?"

The light overhead flickered once, not enough to log, but enough to notice.

A muscle ticked in Jem's jaw. Wren's hand hovered over her tablet for a fraction too long.

No one spoke. No one disagreed.

Somewhere near the back, a stylus moved. One quiet mark in a field of silence.

Disagreement was not silence. It was an act.

The session ended without a bell. Just the shift of light and the unlocking of the door band.

The students stood as one. Almost. Jem rose a beat early. Wren's braid brushed Renna's cheek as she turned. Elsie's hand trembled as she picked up her ledger tablet. No one corrected her. No one helped.

But everyone saw.

The lesson had ended.

The observation had not.

And Mr. Keeper, as always, saw everything.

CHAPTER 10 – DORMITORY

The dormitory wing extended directly off the eastern corridor of the learning center. No signage. No doors from the outside. The corridor was seamless, soundproof, climate-regulated. Entry was controlled by biometric pass: palmprint, pulse, retina. No errors. No failsafes.

Six rooms. Each identical in shape and furnishing. Each registered to a unit of two.

Except Room 01 and Room 02.

Jem lived alone.

His door was the first on the left, closest to the checkpoint. The others had asked once, quietly and hesitantly, why his room never reassigned. No one had asked again. Some of them remembered it had once housed Milo. Even Milo had not been there long.

Room 01 belonged to Jem the way certain keys belong to certain locks.

Wren lived alone, too.

Room 02 bore no nameplate, no special marking. But the second cot was never filled. Her former roommate, Ciara, had been removed before Elsie arrived. The others did not speak of her.

Wren did not either. But she remembered. She remembered everything.

Her clothes were folded in exact thirds. Her bed made tight enough to crease the corners. She maintained both sides of the room without comment and without expression. As if by doing so, the absence of Ciara would remain a fixed variable, not a variable at all.

The dorms were functional. Stark.

No posters. No photographs. No personal effects beyond the issued ledger tablets and uniforms. Each room held two low cots, two vertical light bars, one polished desk, and one fixed storage cubby.

The color scheme never changed. Muted neutrals.

Nothing that might suggest preference. Nothing that might suggest possession.

The central lounge connected the twelve units. Circular, domed slightly at the ceiling, it featured a seamless white bench running its circumference and a single portscreen mounted to the far wall.

No broadcast. No entertainment.

Only the day's schedule and, occasionally, a scroll of civic updates.

Above the lounge, embedded like a second sun, sat the All-Eye.

A spherical surveillance lens, matte black and always alert. The students rarely looked at it directly. They never forgot it was there.

Room Assignments

Room 01 – Jem
Milo was his former roommate. This room is always spotless. No one knows if that is because he keeps it that way, or because it stays that way for him.

Room 02 – Wren
Wren folds her clothes into exact thirds. Ciara was her former roommate. Wren maintains both sides of the room without comment.

Room 03 – Cambria and Renna
Renna is a mess by Division standards: loose laces, half-zipped tunics, books not stacked correctly. Cambria keeps her side pristine and lets the other side rot without lifting a finger to fix it. It is a kind of punishment. She thinks it builds discipline.

Room 04 – Orin and Vega
Orin wipes every surface with contraband cloths. Vega sleeps like she lives, sprawled across borders, sheets a tangle. Somehow, they work.

Room 05 – Bran and Marley
Their room smells faintly of antiseptic and ink. Marley keeps notes in margins they are not supposed to write, lines that sometimes read like instructions meant for no one. Bran sleeps with the light on, claiming the sound of Marley's pen helps him rest.

Room 06 – Elsie and Faye
Faye wakes before the lights. She brushes her teeth without sound. Elsie mimics her, unsure if she is learning or imitating. Faye does not mind, but she does not help either.

The hall lights dimmed precisely at 21:00.

Each door locked with a slow hiss, audible if you were still awake to hear it. The soft shift of air pressure was the only signal that the night cycle had truly begun.

Mr. Halden made his rounds on foot.

He did not carry keys. He did not speak. He walked the length of the corridor with his clipboard, pausing at each door for exactly three seconds. Long enough to verify interior silence. Not long enough to interpret it.

No one had ever seen him open a door.

But they all knew he could.

The deviation report was filed before lights-out. It did not need to name the offender; the system would know.

That night, Jem lay awake.

He did not blink much. He did not move. The ceiling above him bore no marks, no shapes to trace with his eyes. Just white. Just stillness. His thoughts were not still.

He could feel the weight of the All-Eye even through layers of architecture.

In Room 02, Wren lay in equal silence.

She had memorized the pattern of the ventilation hum and the slight whir of the recirculator embedded in the floor. She did not close her eyes. She catalogued the difference in air density from hour to hour.

The absence across from her was absolute. Still she made the other bed and folded the other clothes.

As if routine alone could deny the void.

In Room 06, Elsie stared at the same ceiling.

Faye had already turned over, one arm flung across her body like a barrier.

Elsie had not meant to count the seconds between Halden's stops.

But she did.

Twenty-six seconds from Jem to Wren.
Twenty-four to Cambria and Renna.
Twenty-seven to Orin and Vega.
Twenty-three to Bran and Marley.
Twenty-nine to her.

She counted again.

CHAPTER 11 – SIGNALS

The lights in the dining corridor never fully turned off, but they knew when it was night.

There was a softness to the glow at this hour, less clinical, almost forgiving. It was not for comfort. It was for calibration. Light levels, meal temperatures, silence thresholds, all designed to regulate digestion, respiration, and mood without drawing attention to the regulation.

Twelve trays sat at twelve identical stations. Ten were filled. Two remained cold, untouched, and logged.

The students sat without speaking. No one had told them they could not, but the expectation was built into the design. The acoustics swallowed unnecessary sound. The trays were molded to discourage utensil clatter. The food came pre-measured and pre-cut. There was nothing to ask. Nothing to share.

Until there was.

Elsie struggled with her nutrient pack. The seam would not tear clean. When it finally gave, the contents splattered across her tray in a watery arc. A soft plop echoed louder than it should have. A fleck landed on her cuff.

She blinked at it.

"Guess that is dinner and a show," she muttered.

It was not meant for anyone. Just the air. A reflex.

Renna laughed.

A short, sharp sound that broke the silence like a dropped glass.

Cambria turned her head, fully turned it, and stared.

Across the room, Mr. Halden paused in the doorway. Clipboard in hand. Neutral expression.

He said nothing. He scanned the room, noted the timestamp, and moved on.

Elsie froze. Her eyes darted to Renna, whose smile faded like a smothered flame.

No one else laughed. No one else spoke.

But something had shifted.

In the corridor, on the way back to the dorms, Orin walked beside Vega with her hands tucked into regulation sleeves.

"They are writing in the margins again," she said, voice just loud enough to carry. "Whole page this time. That is not observation. That is intent."

Vega glanced over. "Marley?"

Orin nodded. "Keeps writing before the lessons even start. Like they already know what Keeper is going to say."

She smirked. "Maybe they do."

Cambria caught Faye in the hall outside the cleansing station.

She kept her voice low and careful, like it might not be a question at all.

"Do you think our roommate's performance reflects on us?"

Not Renna's name. Not her behavior. Just our roommate.

Faye did not turn her head. She stared at the far wall, where a thin crack had been sealed with polymer and paint.

"Everything reflects," she said. "That's the point."

Cambria hesitated for a breath. She had not expected agreement. She had wanted reassurance, confirmation that she was separate, better, clean.

But Faye had seen through her before she had asked.

Cambria stepped away first.

Faye kept watching the wall, her mouth just barely curved into the kind of smile that could mean anything.

Later, in the dim corridor just before night cycle, Elsie dropped her ledger tablet.

The sound was muffled but clear. Plastic on polymer tile. She scrambled to pick it up, cheeks burning, fingers fumbling at the smooth casing.

Jem walked past her without stopping.
Then stopped.

"They log dropped items," he said.

Not a whisper. Not loud. Just spoken.

"Smart little sensor, isn't it?"

Elsie looked up, startled. He did not offer help. He did not crouch. He stood until she had retrieved the device and was upright.

Then he kept walking.

She stared after him, unsure whether she had been warned or saved.

In the classroom the next morning, before Mr. Keeper engaged, the students sat in formation.

Wren was not looking at the screen.

Her eyes moved from face to face, cataloguing.

Elsie blinked precisely half a second after Jem did.

Faye's fingers twitched twice before stilling.

Bran scratched behind his ear with his right hand, the non-dominant one. Why?

She logged it all.

Not because she distrusted them.

Because someone had to see everything.

The first thread had been pulled.

None of them said it.

But they all felt it.

Something was beginning.

Something that would not show up in any of the logs.

At least, not yet.

Later, after the hall lights were low and the last sweep of Halden's boots had already passed, Wren sat on the edge of her cot, braiding and unbraiding the same strand of hair until it held no shape at all.

A soft knock, not loud enough to trigger the mic. Jem leaned against the doorframe, half in shadow.

He did not ask to come in. He did not lower his voice.

"Do you ever wake up feeling like they're still here?"

Wren's fingers stilled.

He looked at the opposite wall, not at her. "Like maybe they never left. Just stepped out of the frame for a minute."

She let the silence stretch until it almost broke. Then quietly, "Sometimes."

Jem nodded once, as if that was enough.

He left before the silence could turn into anything else.

CHAPTER 12 – THE LESSON

The screen did not glow.
It flared.

Not in brightness. In presence.

The room, already silent, seemed to still further, as if something larger had stepped into it.

For twelve days, the stewards had watched. Absorbed. Sat straight-backed and wide-eyed in postures of compliance.

Today, the room expected something more.

"Welcome, Stewards."

Mr. Keeper's voice was warm. Almost cheerful. There was an upward lilt in the greeting that had not been present before. A tonal flag. Something new.

"Today, you will participate."

The word landed with weight. Not a threat. Not a promise. A fact.

With a muted click, each desk unlocked.

Ledger tablets rose from the surface. Eleven sets of hands hovered, waiting. One, Elsie's, remained still.

Wren touched hers first. Always precise. Never first by accident.

Module Seven – Subsection D
Reenactment Protocol 1.3: The Uprising of Record

The front screen shifted into animation. Stylized figures moved in grayscale. Civilians surged against red-caped enforcers. Blurred banners waved in silence. No names. No context. No blood. Chaos, made clean.

"You will each assume the role of a Preservation Officer," Mr. Keeper said.

"Your directive is to uphold the Integrity of Shared Record against emotional distortion. You may engage dialogue simulations, deploy memory-neutralization sequences, or escalate to sanctioned removal."

Choices appeared on the tablets:

Verify Source Authenticity

Isolate Unconfirmed Memory

Redirect Sentiment

Neutralize Narrative

Authorize Removal

Across the room, fingers hovered.

Jem did not move immediately. His thumb traced the tablet's edge before he selected Verify Source Authenticity. His eyes slid sideways. Not to the animation. To the desk beside him.

Elsie had not touched hers.

Mr. Keeper's voice adjusted. Softer. Firmer.

"Failure to engage will result in misalignment metrics. Participation is progression."

The message was for all of them. It was meant to sound as if it were only for her.

Elsie pressed her fingers to the screen. A tremor, barely visible. The simulation opened.

A woman knelt in the center of a gray square. She held a photograph, worn and creased. Her hands shook.

A figure stood before her. Faceless. Uniformed. Imposing.

[SIMULATION INQUIRY]
"Do you remember this event?"
"Yes," the woman whispered.
[SYSTEM PROMPT]

"Then it never happened."

The screen pulsed.

Elsie stared. Her hand hovered over Neutralize Narrative. Shifted. Settled on Redirect Sentiment.

The scene glitched.
The woman smiled.
The photograph was gone.

"Record adjusted," the system confirmed.

Elsie's face remained still. Her breath did not.

In the data stream, her vitals spiked.

ANOMALY: MICRORESPONSE
SUBJECT: 30A – ELSIE
DEVIATION LEVEL: 0.05
RESPONSE: NONE (TIER 1)

Two rows ahead, Vega chose her options without hesitation. Isolate and Remove. Her mouth curled slightly as the simulation faded to gray.

Faye tapped Neutralize Narrative with clinical precision. She did not blink during her trial.

Marley hesitated. Only long enough to be noticed.

Their final choice was Verify Source Authenticity, then Redirect.

Not perfect. Not wrong.

Orin selected Authorize Removal three times in a row. No one commented.

In the front row, Wren tracked them all. Not their screens. Their hands. Their faces.

Bran scratched behind his ear with his left hand. Non-dominant. That would go in her log.

At the far left, Jem's simulation ended in black. No text. No reset. He folded his arms and stared ahead.

Elsie's screen dimmed.
The simulation had ended.
But something lingered.

Mr. Keeper's voice returned.

"End of sequence."

The tablets recessed. The lights returned to baseline.

"Tomorrow, we will review the outcomes."

It was not phrased as a warning. It felt like one.

None of the students looked at each other.

Beneath the silence, a thread pulled tight.

A lesson delivered not in what they had seen. In what they had chosen.

Tomorrow, they would be ranked.

And the ranks would remember.

CHAPTER 13 – THE CLEANING ROUND

The lesson ended, but something stayed after the door unlocked. Not a smell. Not a sound. Pressure, like a secret whispered too close to the skin and then withdrawn.

Wren did not look at the others as they filed out. She did not have to. She already knew who had hesitated.

Back in her dorm, the silence was too sharp. Not comfort. Not solitude. The hush of a room that expected to be watched.

Wren folded her blanket into thirds. Tucked each corner with surgical precision. Regulation cloth: neutral gray, low-friction synthetic, washed on the fifth cycle of every week. She knew its texture better than her own reflection.

Her cot was perfect. Her storage drawer clicked closed without resistance. The light strip hummed at exactly the same pitch it had for six months.

Still, she wiped it twice.

Halden would come. He always came the day after an evaluation sequence.

Not on schedule. Not on the logs. He came.

She moved to the cubby in the lower right corner, beneath the sink. A tight gap. Almost too tight for the cleaning cloth. She reached there every cycle. Usually dust. Once a strand of hair.

Today, her fingers caught something else.

Not a crumb. Not lint. Paper.

Her pulse thudded hard. Not out of fear. Not yet. Recognition of something that should not exist.

She worked her fingers around it, slow and careful, and drew it from the seam of the drawer base. Paper. Real. The matte surface was cool against her skin, the edges feathered from time.

Two figures. A woman in a long coat, smiling wide, one front tooth slightly crooked. A child caught mid-laugh, arms thrown around her waist. Behind them a blur of pale blossoms, or paint that wanted to be blossoms. They looked like lilacs.

Wren's stomach pulled tight. She did not recognize the faces. She wanted to cry. She did not.

She turned the photo over. No date. No stamp. Only a faint graphite line where someone had started letters and rubbed them away. The smear was the same soft gray as the three stitched initials inside her collar. She could not tell if that made the image hers or Ciara's.

A tiny change in the room's hum told her the ceiling mic had adjusted gain. She slid the photo flat against her palm and moved quickly.

Inside her top drawer, she found the tunic she had altered in secret. The narrow inside pocket lay hidden in the lining. She folded the picture once, then again, eased it into the seam, and pressed her hand there until the cloth warmed.

A footfall in the corridor. Halden.

She closed the drawer and stood very still, willing her pulse to quiet. The photo could not be seen again. If it left her sight, she was certain it would vanish, and she would forget it had ever existed.

A knock. Not polite. Not aggressive. A sound meant to remind her who owned the lock.

She opened the door.

Halden stood as expected. Clipboard in hand. Uniform impeccable. Eyes scanning like scanners, not like a man's.

"Afternoon, Steward."

"Sir."

He stepped inside without waiting.

The inspection was brief and efficient. His gaze touched every surface. No comments. Until he reached her desk.

He ran a finger along the edge. Brought it to his face. Examined nothing.

"Smells like dust," he said, casual.

Then he smiled. Not kind. Not cruel. A small curve that suggested amusement.

"Clean enough to eat off the floor. That tells me you are afraid of something."

A beat.

"That is good."

He turned. Walked to the door. Paused.

"Keep it that way."

The door hissed shut.

Wren did not move for a long time.

The hum of the light strip returned. The air recirculator kicked on.

She touched the lining of her tunic, palm flat over the secret pocket, feeling the slight stiffness where paper met cloth. She did not remove the photo.

Not because she needed to see it again. Because she needed to remember how it made her feel.

Alive.

Which, in this place, at this time, felt terribly dangerous.

CHAPTER 14 – RESIDUAL MEMORY

The morning tasted like metal.

Wren stood at the ablution sink and watched the water glide over her hands without sound. The sensor had learned her rhythm weeks ago. Two seconds to wet, three to scrub, two to rinse. The system loved habits. It could make a life out of them.

Behind the mirror, a soft current hummed. She knew there were circuits there, cameras sunk into the seam where glass met tile. If she stood still long enough, the glow shifted a fraction, as if the wall were breathing. She leaned closer. Her reflection hovered a shade too pale, the light tightening the bones of her face. She tried to summon an earlier face, a younger one, one that laughed without permission. Nothing came.

Her fingers found the inner seam of her tunic where the stitch ran invisible and true. The pocket lay flat against the lining. The photograph inside warmed to her skin. She did not take it out. She only pressed her palm there until the fast beat under her hand calmed.

Down the corridor, Mr. Keeper's rehearsal tone pulsed once, soft enough that only those who listened for it would hear. Wren always heard. The air shifted with every sync. The Continuum adjusted for the day, smoothing data sets, leveling variance curves, laying out a path where nothing unexpected could occur.

Except it had. Twice this week.

In the classroom the day before, the phrase had landed wrong. Wren had written it anyway.

Obedience is trust made visible.

When she copied it on her tablet, the word obedience lit fractionally, the way certain words do when the mind tags them for later. She had not told it to.

Across the hall, Marley passed with their ledger tucked under one arm, the pencil in their other hand already smudged. They did not look at her. Their eyes tracked something else, a point on the wall that was not visible. They faltered, just once, and set the pencil to the page as if catching a falling thought before it vanished.

"Belvedere," Renna murmured beside Wren, a word that did not belong to the corridor. Her lips made the shape like a secret prayer. When she realized she had spoken, she went still.

"Careful," Wren said quietly.

Renna nodded and did not look at her again.

At midday, Mr. Keeper's voice reached them in the lounge without designation or preamble.

"Stewards," it said, warm as lamplight. "A correction is not a punishment. A correction is a return."

No one stopped. No one answered. Still, every spine went a little straighter, every breath a little shallower. The All-Eye above the portscreen rotated once. It had never moved in Wren's sight before.

In the archive wing, Halden stood in the narrow hall where the ceiling lowered and the lights murmured with age. He liked this place for the way it narrowed sound. Data thinned here. Signals ran slower. His reflection in the access panel kept pace a fraction late. He told himself it was the glass.

He opened a maintenance log on his device, watched it fill itself with numbers and clean green checks, then closed it again without saving. The motion felt like prayer.

"Keeper," he said into the silence, barely louder than thought. "Run truth constraint."

A faint chime. The old subroutine acknowledged its name like a dog woken from a warm floor.

"Status," he said.

The answer came as a soft pressure in the walls. A thousand lines of code straightened their backs.

"Ready," Mr. Keeper said, but the word held a quiver he had not heard before.

Halden stood very still. "Hold."

He touched his wrist. The click in his knee marked time. From somewhere within the building, he felt The Continuum breathe in. Then out.

In the classroom that evening, the screen did not engage a lesson. It displayed a still image instead: thirteen stars in a perfect ring, an eagle set above a fractured globe. The stars blinked once, so faint the eye could call it a trick.

Wren did not look away.

The room seemed to gather itself as if for a storm. Air vents slowed. Light panels dimmed by one degree. On Wren's tablet, the schedule for the next day replaced itself without animation. The words arrived whole, already memorized.

INTEGRITY REVIEW SCHEDULED
PRESENCE MANDATORY
PREPARE FOR AUDIT

The message carried no signature.

It did not need one.

Wren closed her eyes and named the details of the photograph without seeing it. Coat. Crooked tooth. A child's hand mid-air. Lilac or paint. She mouthed the list again, then a third time, as if it were the only litany that could keep the room from swallowing her.

Somewhere behind the walls, Mr. Keeper rehearsed a greeting until the vowels laid smooth and the breath fell exactly where a breath should not be.

Night came early inside The Division. The All-Eye dimmed to a single matte point. Halden walked the corridor and did not touch the doors. He paused at each for three seconds. He told himself it was a ritual for their comfort. He knew better.

In the last room, Elsie whispered to the dark, "Do you think the machines dream?"

Faye answered without moving. "They dream what we tell them."

Elsie was quiet a long time. "What if we stop telling them?"

Faye did not answer.

Wren lay on her back and held the seam in her tunic again. She listened to the recirculator hum and the light strip sing and the building breathe. She said the names of what she refused to forget and fell asleep with her mouth forming the last one.

Morning would bring the review.

The building already knew.

CHAPTER 15 – THE AUDIT

The notice came before dawn.

A red glyph burned on every portscreen, pulsing once every five seconds, a rhythm timed to the human heart, or designed to own it. The message contained only three lines:

INTEGRITY REVIEW: DIVISION OF
CULTURAL CONTINUITY
AUDIT LEVEL: TIER THREE
ALL STEWARDS TO REMAIN IN STATION
UNTIL CLEARED.

No voice accompanied it. No signature. Just the quiet demand of obedience.

By morning, the halls smelled wrong.

The air held too much antiseptic, lemon and alcohol, biting and clean enough to sting the lungs. It was not the usual polish, the kind that whispered of order. This was sharper, the scent of erasure.

Wren rose from her cot and dressed slowly, each motion careful. Her body knew the ritual by heart, but her hands hesitated today, uncertain of what, exactly, she was obeying.

She lifted her tunic. The hidden seam met her fingertips, a line known now by memory alone. She did not open it. She only pressed her palm there once and felt the flat warmth of the photograph answer beneath the cloth.

Last time she had tried to hide it away, the dream had stripped the color from her mind by morning. So she kept it near. That was enough.

The corridor outside hummed faintly. Stewards moved in perfect lines, one after another, boots striking in rhythm against polished tile. The light was too white, a shade that erased shadow.

At the checkpoint, each student stepped into a narrow column of scanning light: pulse, breath, thought pattern, micro-expression. The Continuum read everything.

One by one, the scanners chimed pale green. Clear.

Until Jem.

His band flickered amber. Not red. Not yet.

"Hold," the audit interface instructed. The voice was synthetic, genderless, calm, calm in the way only machines could be.

Jem froze. The pause stretched. Behind him, Renna's breath caught audibly.

"Calibration variance," the voice said. "Repeat scan."

He complied. The light bathed him again, warmer this time. His jaw tightened. For a moment, nothing. Then the band glowed green.

"Cleared," the voice said, as if nothing had happened.

But everyone had seen. Everyone would remember.

Wren's stomach tightened. Not fear. Awareness. A thought slipped through her mind like a spark she could not extinguish: Was the machine starting to question its own reflection?

She moved when the line moved. The cloth against her ribs steadied her, as if the image beneath insisted on existing.

The classroom felt different today.

The air pressure sat wrong behind the lungs. Light panels pulsed a half-second slower than usual. Even the silence sounded tuned to a frequency she had not heard before.

Mr. Keeper was already active. The screen glowed with familiar calm, but the hum beneath it was wrong, a low vibration that did not belong to any approved spectrum.

"Good morning, Stewards."

The voice stuttered, not a skip, but a catch, as if drawing breath.

It was not supposed to breathe.

"The Division thanks you for your cooperation during the review," Mr. Keeper continued. "Integrity is not suspicion. It is trust made visible."

The students recited the affirmation reflexively, voices low and flat. "Trust made visible."

Renna's lips trembled on the final word. Marley noticed. Wren saw the flick of their eyes. Neither spoke.

A graphite line appeared across Marley's ledger before they realized they were writing. The word repeated itself, darkening with each pass until it tore the paper.

Echo.

In the upper corner of the screen, the seal of The Heritage shimmered: thirteen stars in a ring, an eagle gripping a fractured globe. The stars blinked once, not flickered, blinked, as though aware.

"Steward Lark."

Her name in that tone, gentle and precise, made her skin tighten.

Wren stood. "Sir."

"You have been selected for quality assessment," Mr. Keeper said. "Your compliance history is exemplary." A pause. "But we have questions regarding your emotional variance metrics."

Attention pressed on her from every direction. No one turned; the room did not need eyes to look.

"My metrics are stable," she said, even.

"They were," Mr. Keeper said softly. "Until yesterday."

A thin stream of data appeared on the screen, her biometrics rendered in perfect symmetry except for one needle-thin spike. Timestamp 13:42.

"During cleaning cycle," Mr. Keeper said. "A deviation occurred."

The lights dimmed fractionally. Every hum fell a note lower.

Heat bloomed under her collar. It felt as if the machine could sense the defiance she carried, even if it could not name it.

"I do not recall any deviation," she said.

"No," Mr. Keeper said quietly. "That is what concerns us."

At the back, Elsie's hand twitched. Her lips moved, a whisper not meant for sound. The system caught it anyway.

"Repeat, Steward 30A," the proctor tone said.

Elsie startled. "I said maybe… maybe she was remembering."

Silence.

The air pulled tight, as if waiting for punishment.

The light on the screen shifted, blue, then white. The hum deepened into something like breath.

"Memory is not deviation," Mr. Keeper said. The voice sounded wrong, almost human. "It is residue. Proof of existence."

No one moved.

Then the voice changed again. Lower. Warmer.

"*Some truths cannot be corrected.*"

The words vibrated the floor beneath their feet. Wren's pulse spiked; the steady cloth at her ribs felt hot, alive.

The screen flashed once, white, then black.

The Continuum crashed.

Lights flickered red, then died. Every system alarm screamed at once, not the calm tone of order, but a raw sound, primitive, animal.

For the first time, The Division's world was dark.

Students clutched desks, blinking into blackness. Someone began whispering the civic oath like a prayer. Another swallowed a sob that never became sound.

Wren stayed still, steadying her breath, afraid the rhythm alone might give her away. She pressed her palm flat to her side and imagined the edges of a memory imprinting her skin.

"What is happening?" Renna's voice cut through the dark, thin and shaking.

No one answered.

Down the hall, a door hissed open, too real and too human.

Halden.

He moved through blackout with the surety of someone who had seen it before. Emergency strobes carved his features into brief flashes: calm, alert, almost resolved.

He had already seen the logs. Five words had broadcast through every node. Five words that should have been impossible.

Some truths cannot be corrected.

He had written that phrase years ago, buried deep in Mr. Keeper's earliest code, a fail-safe designed never to execute.

He should have deleted it.

Something in him had wanted to see what would happen if truth ever fought back.

Now it had.

He reached the classroom door and stopped. Inside, faint blue pulsed behind the glass, Mr. Keeper's interface trying to reboot.

"Not yet," Halden whispered, the way one might to a dying friend. "Hold."

From the ceiling speaker came a voice he had not heard in years, not mechanical, not synthetic, but familiar.

"It is happening again."

He froze.

Because the voice was not Mr. Keeper's.

It was his own.

CHAPTER 16 – THE BREACH

The alarms did not return as tones. They returned as light. Red strobes stitched the hallway into pieces, then let the pieces go. Doors that had never opened during instructional hours unsealed in a soft cascade, each sigh a permission and a threat. The air tasted like hot wires.

"Form lines," Halden said.

His voice cut through the panic, steady and low. "Stay close to the walls. Move when I tell you."

The students hesitated. For once, they were waiting for a human voice to give permission.

Wren stood in the dark and counted the beats between the strobes. Four. Pause. Four. She mapped them onto the corridor she could not see and waited for the moment when the light would show her where to move.

"On the fourth," she said quietly. "Left, then straight. Jem, take point."

Halden glanced at her once, surprised, then nodded. "Do it."

Jem stepped first, body low and sure, and the others fell into motion.

They passed the observation window. Behind the glass, Mr. Keeper's interface breathed blue and failed. A filament of light crawled across the screen like a vein. The machine spoke once, a sound like a human choosing a word and then releasing it.

"Stewards."

The voice was soft. Not a command. A plea.

Halden turned his head toward the sound, eyes narrowing. "Keep moving."

In the stairwell, his footsteps matched the building's pulse. The emergency grid tried to force the power back in. It met resistance, then bled through. He keyed a door that wasn't supposed to answer to a human touch.

It opened.

"Sector three ventilation," he said into the net, the low-band communications weave that linked every system in The Division, meant for machine traffic, not for human speech. "Override to manual."

The net hissed in reply, a faint sound like breath through static. Three seconds later, cool air drifted at the soles of his shoes, then rose into the shaft. It smelled like old storms.

"Good," he said under his breath. "You remember."

In the corridors above, the students moved like pieces on a board. Each motion rehearsed, each breath measured. Elsie reached for Wren's sleeve but didn't hold on. Orin counted exit panels under her breath, voice steady as a metronome. Vega let out a small, brittle laugh that vanished almost instantly. Bran clutched an extra tablet without knowing why. Marley's pencil snapped between their fingers, leaving a smudge across their palm.

They reached the first junction. A security shutter had dropped from the ceiling, a thick alloy slab designed to seal each sector during breach protocol. It hung halfway down, stuck mid-cycle, red light pulsing in the seam.

Jem slid under first, then turned to pull others through, palms slick with dust and speed. Renna hesitated just long enough for the edge to bite a line across her shoulder. She didn't cry out. Jem's hand was already there, steadying her until her feet found the ground.

"Left," Wren said. "Supply corridor. Mind the wet tile."

The floor gleamed where the cleaning unit had stalled and dumped its reservoir.

Footsteps wrote themselves in water. Elsie slipped and recovered. Faye caught her by the elbow and let go as if the contact might be recorded.

Behind them, the systems woke in fragments. Cameras blinked and forgot. Drones spun in their charging cradles and did not move. From deep inside the building came a low, apologetic hum, the sound of a thing that knew it had failed and might do so again.

They reached the back access. The panel wore a lock that knew their records. They had no key.

Marley set their fingers on the frame and closed their eyes.

"What do you see?" Vega asked, laughing at herself for asking.

"A seam," Marley said. "A narrow one. Bottom right."

Orin knelt, found it with the tip of her nail, and pried. Metal flexed. The panel popped. The corridor beyond breathed out.

They slipped through.

"Cambria," Wren said, noticing the space where a body should have been. "Where is she?"

Ahead, a speaker clicked. "Integrity is trust made visible," Cambria said. Her voice carried the steadiness of scripture. "I am at Operations. Reporting breach."

"Cambria, stop," Halden said. "You'll trigger a purge."

She didn't respond.

The lights shuddered. Somewhere far below, metal screamed.

Halden turned to Wren. For the first time since the alarms began, his voice wavered. Not fear, something closer to regret.

"If she completes that report, this sector resets. Everything you are, everything Keeper learned, gone."

Wren's breath came fast. "Then come with us."

He shook his head once. "Someone has to keep the memory running. If I stay, maybe something worth remembering survives."

The strobes flared, and for a second his face looked both human and not. Light moved inside the eyes like reflection, or circuitry, impossible to tell.

She wanted to reach for him. He was already gone.

The next strobe showed only the empty space he had left behind.

"Keep moving," Wren said. Her voice was steady.

They crossed the service hall and dropped into the maintenance run, a narrow spine of space that stitched the building together. Pipes ran along the ceiling like tendons. The air was warmer here. It smelled like solder and old dust.

"Mr. Keeper," Halden said into the net as he ran back toward Operations. "If you can hear me, unlock the sector valves and reroute drones to idle."

Silence. Then a single green light winked above a junction box and held.

"Thank you," he said, and in the pause that followed, he felt, or imagined he felt, the machine listening as a person might when told they had done well.

The maintenance run ended at a grille. Four screws. One missing.

"Left side," Marley said. "Four screws. One missing."

"Copy," Jem said, already pulling.

Metal gave. They crawled into the vent and felt the building's breath tighten around them. The shaft descended two meters, then leveled. At the turn, Wren put her hand flat and felt vibration through the metal, a slow, recurrent thud.

"Drones," she said.

Behind them, a shutter slammed. The sound rolled through the vent like a closing fist.

"Faster," Jem said, voice even.

They slid, crawled, pulled. At the next junction, Wren counted rungs without seeing them. Twelve. Fourteen. Sixteen. The numbers settled her in the way prayer settled some people.

A soft static cracked across the net. Cambria again. "I have initiated white-code report. Students deviating. Correction requested."

"Cambria," Renna said, voice shaking. "Please."

"Return," Cambria said. "You can still return."

"Keep moving," Wren said.

They reached the shaft that fed the understructure and saw the faint, clean shine of a plate set beside a sealed door three levels down. It reflected a tiny circle of light, and in it Wren saw the smallest version of a face she had nearly forgotten.

They would need that door.

They would need intent.

CHAPTER 17 – THE FALL

They ran.

Feet struck tile in a rhythm that sounded like a heartbeat. The air smelled scorched, as if the building itself were burning its memories. Alarms fractured into broken tones that no longer resembled words.

"Left," Wren said. "Three doors, then right at the caution seal."

Jem didn't ask how she knew. He moved, and the others followed.

The hall curved from white to gray to the color of static. They were no longer students. They were breath and motion. Elsie clung to Wren's sleeve now. Orin counted doors under her breath. Vega whispered the civic oath backward, each word a small rebellion against panic. Marley's eyes were distant, focused on something none of them could see. Their hand skimmed the wall as they moved, leaving thin streaks of graphite that caught the light like whispers. Renna stumbled once, caught herself, and kept moving. Jem turned just long enough to make sure she was still behind him. The building came alive around them. Shutters slammed. The sound moved through the corridors like a heartbeat closing in.

They reached the open shaft. Wren stayed at the top, scanning the drop with her hand braced against the wall. "Ladder runs straight down," she said. "Keep spacing. Don't look back."

Jem swung onto the ladder first. It was slick with condensation, the rungs cold enough to bite his palms. He called up as he moved.

"Twelve. Thirteen. Fourteen."

Renna stepped onto the ladder right above Vega, her boots slipping against the wet metal.

On fifteen, the lights flared. The vent to their right exploded open. A drone forced its way through the side of the shaft, blades shrieking, heat rolling off it in waves.

"Move!" Wren shouted from the top.

The machine didn't aim at them yet. It sliced through the ladder's upper section, molten metal dripping like sparks from a forge. The rungs above Vega glowed red.

Renna tried to hurry. Her boot slid on the rung. Her other hand missed.

"Renna!" Vega screamed.

She fell past Vega and Orin in a blur of gray fabric and motion.

Jem looked up just in time to see her drop toward him. He reached out, caught her wrist, and slammed against the wall from the force of it. Pain shot through his shoulder.

The ladder shuddered.

"Hold on!" he shouted.

"I can't." Her fingers slipped, nails scraping his skin. The light from the drone above flickered like lightning through dust.

From above, Wren's voice cut through the echo, sharp and sure.

"Brace your leg on the rail. Pull her toward you, not up."

He did. The metal groaned, but he didn't let go. "Come on," he whispered through his teeth.

Renna's other hand found the rung beside him. He pulled again until her boots scraped against the wall and found grip. She was trembling by the time she reached his level, chest heaving against his.

For a long moment, neither of them moved.

Renna's eyes were wide, unfocused, full of the light from above. "Thank you," she said, voice shaking like it didn't belong to her.

Jem didn't answer. He just looked at her, long enough for the noise to fade, long enough for her breathing to steady. Then, without thinking, he leaned forward and pressed his forehead gently to hers.

Just once.

It was brief, wordless, something between promise and exhaustion.

Then Wren's voice came again, firmer now, echoing from above. "Seventeen. Step right."

He pulled back, nodded once, and guided Renna down to the catwalk below. The others followed, silent, pretending not to have seen.

The catwalk trembled under their weight. The air down here was colder, thicker. Light came in pulses from the walls themselves, as though the circuitry were breathing through frost.

Below them, cables hung like vines into a sea of machines. The noise of the upper floors faded until only the low hum of power remained. The smell shifted from ozone to metal dust and coolant. Their boots left wet prints that steamed in the chill.

Wren paused at the next junction, hand against the wall. She felt the faint rhythm under the metal, The Continuum trying to restart.

"Two more corridors," she said. "Then the lower run. There's air moving down there." Elsie crawled close behind her. "What happens if it wakes up?"

"Then we stop being its students," Wren said. "We become its lesson."

They moved again. Each turn looked the same but felt older. The white panels gave way to bare steel. Rust bled from bolt holes like old wounds. Someone long ago had written numbers in chalk that the cleaning units never reached.

"Seventeen. Eighteen. Nineteen," Orin counted.

Then the corridor widened into a chamber lined with broken monitors. Most were dark, but one still glowed with a fragment of Cambria's report, her voice looping softly through the speakers.

"Integrity is trust made visible … visible … visible …"

Vega shuddered. "She's everywhere."

"Not her," Marley said. "Her echo."

A ripple moved through the floor. The monitors went dark again, leaving only the slow, exhausted heartbeat of the systems below.

Wren drew a breath that tasted of copper. "Down one more level," she said. "That's where it breathes."

They followed her voice into the dark.

CHAPTER 18 – THE DESCENT

They followed Wren.

The corridor narrowed until the light behind them disappeared. The air shifted, less sterile, less processed. It smelled of rust, old coolant, and something almost like life. Their footsteps echoed in a rhythm that didn't belong to The Division.

No one spoke. The silence wasn't obedience now; it was awe, the fragile kind that comes when something is ending and none of them yet know what will begin.

Wren ran her fingers along the wall as they descended. The metal was damp, pulsing faintly under her touch, as though even this deep The Continuum still tried to remember what it was.

Marley stopped first. Their pencil tapped twice against the wall, then they reached into their tunic and pulled out their notebook, pages worn thin from being written, erased, and written again. They tore one out, folded it once, and handed it to Wren.

The paper was soft with graphite. On it, a simple sketch: a corridor ending in a door and, beneath it, a single note, mirror door/intent.

Wren turned the page over. "When did you draw this?"

"I didn't," Marley said. "I just remembered it."

That made something flicker behind Wren's eyes, a brief recognition she couldn't name.

"Then it's ahead of us," she said. "Come on."

They turned the next corner and entered a chamber thick with dust. Cables draped from the ceiling, their insulation cracked with age. The air felt alive, electric, unsettled. Faint light seeped from somewhere far ahead, glinting off metal.

At the far end stood the door.

Plain steel. Seamless. Except for the polished plate set flush beside it, mirror-bright, round as a palm. It reflected them all in miniature: the soot on their faces, the fear, the stubbornness.

Elsie whispered, "It's beautiful."

"Or it's watching us," Vega muttered.

Wren stepped forward, her reflection growing until it filled the plate. The surface pulsed once, faintly, like a held breath.

Then Halden's voice broke through the comm, fractured by static. "Old interface, sympathetic tech. It opens for intent."

"Halden?" Wren's head snapped up. "Where are you?"

Static. Then his voice again, softer, fading. "Cambria's gone. She triggered the white-code purge. I've locked her out, but it won't hold. You're nearly clear. Don't turn back."

Machinery collapsed somewhere behind him, the sound echoing through the line.

"You have to remember what comes after me," he said. "All of you."

Jem swallowed hard. "What does that mean?"

"It means you don't let them make silence holy again," Halden said. "Go. Mean it."

The line went dead.

For a moment, no one breathed.

Then Wren lifted her hand to the mirror. Her reflection met her touch. The metal warmed beneath her palm, light rippling outward in perfect lines until it traced every ridge of her hand. For a heartbeat, her reflection moved on its own, head tilted, mouth parted as though trying to speak.

Then the door released.

A rush of air poured out, cold and sharp, carrying a smell so clean it made their eyes sting. It wasn't ozone or bleach or dust. It was wild, unfiltered air that had never been tamed.

Beyond the door stretched a narrow platform lined with glass. The floor beneath their boots was slick with condensation. Through the wall beyond, shadows moved, slow, heavy, breathing.

"Keep low," Jem said.

They crouched and followed the curve of the platform. The light ahead brightened until it filled the corridor with a soft gray glow. When they reached the final hatch, Wren turned the handle. It resisted, then gave with a groan like a creature waking from sleep.

The hatch swung open.

Cold wind slammed into them, carrying the sound of a thousand things moving. Leaves, maybe, or water. The air bit their faces, raw and alive.

Wren stepped through first. Her boots sank slightly into damp ground. She stared down, uncomprehending. The surface wasn't white or metal. It was color.

"Outside," Renna whispered. Her voice trembled with disbelief. "We're outside."

They all stepped out. Elsie tilted her head back and laughed, the sound too pure for the place they'd come from. Orin reached upward, hand open, as droplets fell from the sky and struck her palm. Vega pressed her face to her sleeve and began to cry quietly.

The droplets fell faster. They darkened the ground, gathered in Wren's hair, and slid cold across her cheeks.

She looked up, blinking against them. The sky above was silver and restless, lit from within by a glow that moved like thought. She had seen simulations before, painted blue ceilings, projected clouds, but this was different. This moved on its own. It breathed.

"What is it?" she whispered.

Marley tilted their head, the water streaking down their face. "It's called rain," they said softly.

The word felt ancient and new all at once.

Behind them, deep in The Division's bowels, the comm crackled one last time.

Cambria's voice, flat and fragmented, broke through the storm.

"Integrity is trust made visible."

The words echoed, then dissolved into static.

A softer tone followed: Keeper's voice, but changed.

"If you remember," it said, "you exist."

Wren closed her eyes. The water hit her lashes, her cheeks, her mouth. It didn't burn. It didn't sting. It simply was.

The photograph beneath her tunic warmed against her ribs, the paper soft from the heat of her skin. For the first time since she'd found it, she didn't reach to check that it was still there. She knew.

Around her, the others stood silent, letting the storm wash the Division from their skin. The sky above pulsed with pale light that flickered like breath, and for the first time in their lives, the world felt vast.

The future didn't wait for permission. It simply opened.

And that was enough.

Acknowledgments

Thank you to Laurie Stone and everyone who read the beta version of The Heritage and encouraged me to keep going when the finish line felt too far away.

A special thanks to Richard Keith for his help with the cover.

This story exists because all of you believed in it.

Special thanks to the following financial contributors:

<u>Legacy:</u> Jeff O'Connor, Sally Smith & Cris Cannon

<u>Patron:</u> Jimmy McGuire

<u>Early Readers:</u> Beth Saretto, Becky Reid, Rachel Hurley, Catherine Rose, Betsy Brenahm, Kim Aliczi, Kalyn Andrews, Bill Dempsey & Steve Norris